A PRIMARY SOURCE
LIBRARY OF
AMERICAN CITIZENSHIP ™

The Supreme Court and
the Judicial Branch

Anne Beier

rosen central
Primary Source™

The Rosen Publishing Group, Inc., New York

Published in 2004 by The Rosen Publishing Group, Inc.
29 East 21st Street, New York, NY 10010

Copyright © 2004 by The Rosen Publishing Group, Inc.

First Edition

Library of Congress Cataloging-in-Publication Data

Beier, Anne.
The Supreme Court and the judicial branch/Anne Beier.—1st ed.
    p. cm.—(A Primary source library of American citizenship)
Summary: Introduces the American court system and how the Supreme Court decides the constitutionality of laws. Includes bibliographical references and index.
ISBN 0-8239-4478-6 (library binding)
1. United States. Supreme Court—Juvenile literature. 2. Judicial power—United States—Juvenile literature. 3 Judicial review—United States—Juvenile literature. 4. Judicial process—United States—Juvenile literature. [1. United States Supreme Court.]
I. Title. II. Series.
KF8742.Z9B45 2004
347.73'26—dc22

                                                                    2003013365

Manufactured in the United States of America

On the cover: Above right, a portrait of John Jay, the first chief justice of the United States Supreme Court. Below left, an official photograph of the current justices of the Supreme Court.

Photo credits: cover (background), p. 23 © The Library of Congress Manuscript Division; cover (top right), p. 7 © New York Historical Society/Bridgeman Art Library; cover (bottom left), p. 30 Photograph by Richard Strauss, Smithsonian Institution, Courtesy of the Supreme Court of the United States; p. 4 © Joseph Sohm, Visions of America/Corbis; p. 5 © Records of the Continental and Confederation Congresses and the Constitutional Convention, 1174-1789, Record Group 360, National Archives; pp. 8, 9 © Reuters NewMedia Inc./Corbis; pp. 10, 19, 21 © AFP/Corbis; p. 11 © Myung J. Chun-Pool/Getty Images; p. 13 (left) © Treaties and Other International Agreements, Series #5433, General Records of the United States Government, Record Group 11, National Archives; p. 13 (right) © Brooks Kraft/Corbis; p. 14 © Susan Steinkamp/Corbis; p. 15 (top) © Bettmann/Corbis; p. 15 (bottom) © Pat Cunningham/Corbis Sygma; p. 16 © Brett Coomer/Getty Images; pp. 17, 18, 20, 22, 25, 27, 29 (bottom) © AP/Wide World Photos; p. 24 © Wally McNamee/Corbis; p. 29 (top) © Records of the Supreme Court of the United States, Record Group 267, National Archives

Designer: Tahara Hasan; Photo Researcher: Amy Feinberg

Contents

America's Highest Court

Laws are needed to keep an orderly society. The Constitution is the basis of our laws and our legal system. The authors of the Constitution created the Supreme Court. Federal and state court systems operate under the Supreme Court. The courts protect citizens and our country and punish those who violate the law. The Supreme Court interprets the laws to make sure they comply with the rights given to citizens in the Constitution.

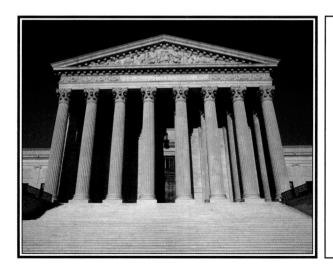

This is the facade of the United States Supreme Court Building in Washington, D.C. It was designed in the neoclassical style to resemble the Parthenon on the Acropolis in Athens, Greece.

The Constitution of the United States of America, drafted in 1787 and ratified by the states in 1789, established the Supreme Court and its independence from the other branches of government.

The Supreme Court is the highest and most powerful court in America. The Constitution created the Supreme Court in 1789. The Constitution was created to bond the colonies together under one government with one common body of law. When colonies became states, each state wanted its own laws. But state laws cannot conflict with the laws of the Constitution.

The First Chief Justice

John Jay was the first chief justice of our country. He served from 1789 to 1795. At that time, the Supreme Court was located in New York City.

This is a portrait of John Jay, the first chief justice of the United States Supreme Court.

Our judicial system tries cases in either criminal or civil courts. Criminal trials occur when a state or federal law has been broken. A person is accused of committing a crime. A judge and jury listen to the facts. A verdict of guilty or not guilty is made, usually by the jury, but sometimes by the judge.

In this Florida courtroom scene in 2000, lawyers for presidential candidates Al Gore and George W. Bush present testimonies regarding contested votes in the counting of the state's ballots.

Judge Nikki Clark in Tallahassee, Florida, listens to lawyers' arguments regarding ballot counting in the 2000 presidential election.

A civil case occurs when someone brings a lawsuit against someone else. The plaintiff, the accuser, claims that the defendant has caused him or her harm in some way. A judge and a jury hear the facts presented by lawyers, who are trained to know the law and the rules of presenting evidence. If the defendant is found guilty, he or she must correct the injury or damage, or pay for the plaintiff's losses.

Steve Zach *(left)*, attorney for Al Gore, and Phil Beck, attorney for George W. Bush, present arguments in a Florida courtroom regarding the contested 2000 presidential election.

Los Angeles Police Department detective Robert Bub presents evidence to the jury in a Van Nuys, California, courtroom in actor Robert Blake's murder trial in 2003.

2 How the Legal System Works

Courts work in different jurisdictions, that is, different states or regions of the country. They make sure our citizens and our government obey the laws. International laws must be followed, too. When Congress ratifies, or votes to approve, a treaty the president has negotiated with another nation, that treaty becomes part of American law.

Across From the Capitol

The Supreme Court Building is located across the street from the Capitol Building, where Congress meets. The address is The Supreme Court, 1st Street, Washington, D.C. 20543.

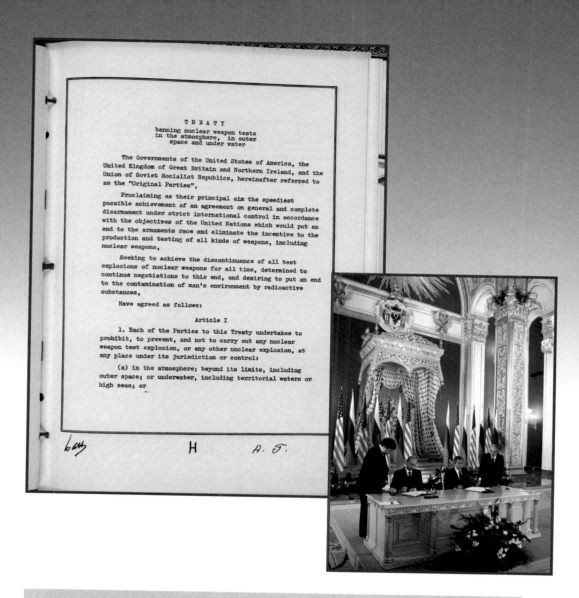

Above, the draft of the 1963 Limited Test Ban Treaty between the United States, Great Britain, and the former Soviet Union. Below, in 2002, George W. Bush and Vladimir Putin sign another treaty limiting strategic nuclear warheads.

Federal cases begin in one of 90 to 94 U.S. district courts. The country is divided into districts. The number changes from time to time as the population changes. Federal cases can be between two parties, or between a party and the state or the federal government. Questions about constitutional rights are tried in federal district courts, too.

President George H. W. Bush delivers his 1990 State of the Union speech to a joint session of Congress.

Above, in 1959, Frankie Carbo, a convicted defendant in a prize-fighting corruption case, leaves a United States district court, where his appeal was heard. Below, U.S. district court judge James Parker is pictured in his courtroom in Albuquerque, New Mexico, in 1998.

A person can appeal a verdict if he or she thinks it is unfair. Usually, however, a person cannot simply claim that a verdict was wrong and demand another trial. He or she must argue that the law was applied unfairly, or that there was an error in the way the trial was conducted or the way evidence was used.

Rusty Hardin, an attorney representing the Arthur Andersen accounting firm in the 2002 Enron scandal, enters a Houston courtroom to begin jury selection.

A statue of Robert Livingston in the lobby of the New York State Court of Appeals. Livingston was the first chancellor of the Court for the Trial of Impeachments and the Correction of Errors, the predecessor of the appellate court.

A federal case is appealed to the next highest court, the U.S. Court of Appeals. There are eleven U.S. Circuit Courts of Appeals. Appeals courts have three or more judges. They decide if the federal district court's verdict was fair. Appeals courts have the power to change the decision. Then either of the parties can appeal to the Supreme Court.

Attorney David Bois, representing Napster, holds a press conference at the federal courtroom where he appealed a decision preventing the company from distributing electronic music files.

Above are the justices of the U.S. Court of Appeals for the District of Columbia, who in 2001 decided the antitrust suit brought by the government against Microsoft.

The state court system works much like the federal court system. The state courts also decide criminal and civil matters. The jury process is used most often in state courts. There are superior courts where trials are first held, and then there are state appeals courts and a state supreme court. Beyond that, a person can appeal a decision to the U.S. Supreme Court.

U.S. attorney Jim Letten gives a press conference on the steps of the U.S. Court of Appeals for the Fifth Circuit in New Orleans.

Justices of the Florida Supreme Court hear arguments from Democratic and Republican lawyers about the hand recounting of ballots during the 2000 presidential election.

3 Inside the Supreme Court

Nine justices serve on the Supreme Court. There is one chief justice and eight associate justices. Their decisions are final. Supreme Court justices are appointed for life. A justice can retire, be impeached, or die during that time. The president then appoints a new judge. The Senate has to approve the president's choice.

President Bill Clinton presents Ruth Bader Ginsburg, his nominee for Supreme Court justice, in 1993.

A copy of the 1789 memorandum written by President George Washington nominating the first justices of the Supreme Court. There were six justices at the time.

The Supreme Court is asked to hear about 5,000 cases each year. Only about 150 cases are chosen. It takes only four judges to agree to hear the case. First, the lawyers for the two parties present a brief. This is a statement of why each party feels that the decision of the lower courts did not follow the law. Each party has an hour and a half to present its case. The lawyers may be asked questions by the justices. There is no jury.

Members of the Senate Judiciary Committee conduct hearings on the nomination of Clarence Thomas to the Supreme Court in 1991.

Supreme Court justice nominee Clarence Thomas is sworn in before the Senate Judiciary Committee that ultimately confirmed his appointment.

The nine justices then meet in private to review the case. No records are kept of their private conversations. A vote is taken and the majority, that is, at least five of the justices, decide the merits of the appeal. One of the justices writes the majority opinion. Other justices can write a concurring opinion. A justice who disagrees can write a dissenting opinion. The majority decision then becomes a precedent for the interpretation of the law in the lower courts.

The First Woman Justice

Sandra Day O'Connor was the first woman to serve on the Supreme Court. She was appointed in 1981 and is still an associate justice.

In 1981, Chief Justice Warren Burger swears in Sandra Day O'Connor as a Supreme Court associate justice.

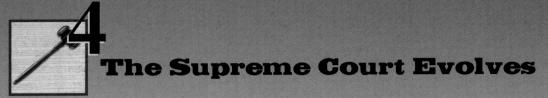

4 The Supreme Court Evolves

The Supreme Court has grown and changed since its creation. In 1896, in the case known as *Plessy v. Ferguson*, the Court decided that the states could segregate black and white students in separate schools as long as their educational advantages were equal. But in 1954, in *Brown v. Board of Education*, the Supreme Court changed its mind. It ruled that segregated schools could never be equal. Future Court cases will test new laws to keep current with a changing world.

The First Black Justice

Justice Thurgood Marshall was the first black American to serve on the Supreme Court. He served from 1967 to 1991. In 1954, Marshall was the lawyer who argued against segregated schools before the Court in *Brown v. Board of Education*.

Above, the first page of the 1954 Supreme Court decision in *Brown v. Board of Education*, the historic decision that ended segregation of schools. Below, on the steps of the Supreme Court, attorneys George Hayes, Thurgood Marshall, and James Nabrit, who argued the case, congratulate each other.

The composition of the Court also changes as some justices retire or die. The chief justice sits in the center behind the bench. The newest justice sits at the left end. When a new justice is appointed, each justice changes his or her seat. Their seats move left to right as they become more senior.

The current justices of the Supreme Court. Seated are Sandra Day O'Connor and John Paul Stevens. Standing from left to right are Anthony M. Kennedy, Antonin Scalia, William H. Rehnquist, David Souter, Ruth Bader Ginsburg, Clarence Thomas, and Stephen G. Breyer.

Glossary

appeal (uh-PEEL) To ask a higher court for a decision to be changed.
brief (BREEF) An outline of the main arguments of a legal case.
concur (kuhn-KUR) To agree with.
defendant (di-FEN-duhnt) A person in a court case who has been accused of a crime or is being sued.
dissent (di-SENT) To disagree with an idea or opinion.
international (in-tur-NASH-uh-nuhl) Between two or more nations. Involving different countries.
interpret (in-TUR-prit) To decide what something means.
jury (JUR-ee) A group of people at a trial who listens to the evidence and decides whether the person accused of a crime is innocent or guilty.
lawyer (LAW-yur) A person who is trained to advise people about the law and who acts and speaks for them in court.
plaintiff (PLAYN-tif) A party who takes legal action against another.
precedent (PREH-suh-dehnt) A first principle, which others use to decide how to interpret a law.
senior (SEE-nyur) Older or oldest, or longest serving.
trial (TRYL) The examination of evidence in a court of law to decide if a charge or claim is true.
verdict (vur-DIKT) The decision of a jury or judge to determine if an accused person is guilty or not guilty.

Web Sites

Due to the changing nature of Internet links, the Rosen Publishing Group, Inc., has developed an online list of Web sites related to the subject of this book. This site is updated regularly. Please use this link to access the list:

http://www.rosenlinks.com/pslac/scjb

Primary Source Image List

Page 4: The United States Supreme Court building, photographed by Joseph Sohm in 1990.
Page 5: United States Constitution, now at the National Archives.
Page 8: A courtroom in the Leon County Courthouse, December 3, 2000, photographed by Tim Sloan for Reuters.
Page 9: Judge Nikki Clark, photographed by Tim Sloan for Reuters, 2000.

Page 10: Steve Zach and Phil Beck, photographed by Chang Lee for the *New York Times*, 2000.
Page 11: Los Angeles Police Department detective Robert Bub, photographed by Myung J. Chun, 2003.
Page 13 (top): The 1963 Limited Test Ban Treaty, now in the National Archives.
Page 13 (bottom): George W. Bush and Vladimir Putin in Moscow, 2002, photographed by Brooks Kraft.
Page 14: George H.W. Bush before Congress, photographed by Susan Steinkamp, 1990.
Page 15 (bottom): Judge James Parker, photographed by Pat Cunningham, 1998.
Page 16: Rusty Hardin, photographed by Brett Coomer, 2002.
Page 17: Statue of Robert Livingston, photographed by Jim McKnight for the Associated Press, 1997.
Page 18: David Bois, photographed by Dan Krauss for the Associated Press, 2000.
Page 19: The U.S. Court of Appeals for the District of Columbia, photographed by Luke Frazza, 2001.
Page 20: U.S. Attorney Jim Letten, photographed by Bill Haber for the Associated Press, 2002.
Page 21: Florida Supreme Court, photographed by Allison Long, 2000.
Page 22: Bill Clinton and Ruth Bader Ginsburg, photographed by Doug Mills for the Associated Press, 1993.
Page 23: George Washington's nominations for Supreme Court, 1789, now in the manuscript division of the Library of Congress.
Page 24: Senate Judiciary Committee, photographed by Wally McNamee, 1991.
Page 25: Clarence Thomas, photographed by John Duricka for the Associated Press, 1991.
Page 27: Warren Burger and Sandra Day O'Connor, photographed by Michael Evans for the Associated Press, 1981.
Page 29 (top): *Brown v. Board of Education of Topeka*, now with the Records of the Supreme Court of the United States, National Archives.
Page 29 (bottom): George Hayes, Thurgood Marshall, and James Nabrit, Associated Press photograph, 1954.

Index

About the Author

Anne Beier is a freelance writer who lives in upstate New York.